Lola
at the
Library

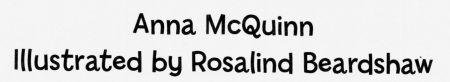

Anna McQuinn
Illustrated by Rosalind Beardshaw

SCHOLASTIC INC.

New York   Toronto   London   Auckland   Sydney
Mexico City   New Delhi   Hong Kong   Buenos Aires

Lola loves Tuesdays.
On Tuesdays Lola and her
mommy go to the library.

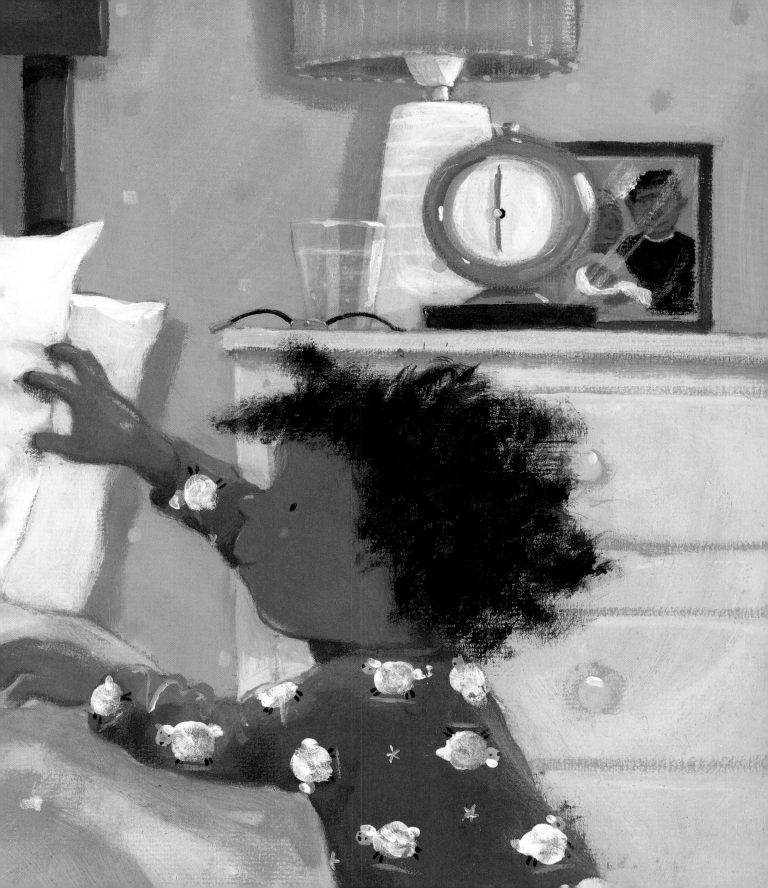

The library opens at nine o'clock,
but Lola is ready to go
long before that!

She puts all the books she borrowed
last week in her backpack.

Her library card is also *very* important.

The library is not very
far away, so Lola and
her mommy always walk there.

Lola and her mommy give back
the books from last week. The librarian
buzzes them through the machine.

There is a special section in the library just for children.

It is really cool.
Nobody ever says, "Shhh!"

Sometimes there is singing.

Lola knows all the words
and the hands for
"Twinkle, Twinkle, Little Star."

Sometimes there is storytime.
Lola loves that.

After storytime Lola chooses
her books. In the library
she can have *any* book she wants.

Lola likes stories with bears
and *anything* with shoes.
There are so many,
it takes ages to choose!

Mommy has some books, too.
The librarian buzzes them
through the machine,
then stamps the date inside.

Lola must bring them
back in two weeks.
But she will probably be back
for more long before then!

Lola and her mommy always get
a snack after visiting the library.
Mommy has a cappuccino,
and Lola has juice.

Whenever Lola has been good, her mommy lets her taste the foam—mmmmm!

Then it is time to go home again.

Every night, after Lola is tucked in bed,
her mommy reads her a story.

It is the *best* way to end the day.

Dedicated with thanks to Rana, Malika, Noor, Angel, Zhara, Hassan, Ashleigh, Shannon, Mathilde, Tabitha, Honor, Anastasia, Alexandro, Alejo, Oscar, Benjamin, Max, Nawaal, Philmon, Nahome, Matthew, Sabri, Caitlin, Katie, Zak, and all the regulars in the Acton Library Family Book Group; to Zaynab and Milgo for helping with the research; to Abir for not complaining all the mornings Sally woke her up early to come to the Book Group; and to Husain for sharing my cappuccino—A. M.

To Philippa, with love—R. B.

ISBN-13: 978-0-545-00290-5
ISBN-10: 0-545-00290-7

Text copyright © 2006 by Anna McQuinn.
Illustrations copyright © 2006 by Rosalind Beardshaw.
All rights reserved. Published by Scholastic Inc., 557 Broadway, New York, NY 10012, by arrangement with Charlesbridge Publishing. SCHOLASTIC and associated logos are trademarks and/or registered trademarks of Scholastic Inc.

12 11 10 9 8 7 6 5 4 3 2 1   7 8 9 10 11/0

Printed in the U.S.A.   40

First Scholastic printing, January 2007

Illustrations done in acrylic on paper
Display type and text type set in Garamouche Bold and Billy